TAILS from History

A Raccoon at the White House

By Rachel Dougherty
Illustrated by Rachel Sanson

Ready-to-Read

Simon Spotlight
New York London Toronto Sydney New Delhi

Dedicated to Laurie and to my critique group for helping this story grow and finding it a home —R. D.

For my dad —R. S.

SIMON SPOTLIGHT
An imprint of Simon & Schuster Children's Publishing Division
1230 Avenue of the Americas, New York, New York 10020
This Simon Spotlight edition December 2019

For information about special discounts for bulk purchases, please contact Simon & Schuster Special Sales at 1-866-506-1949 or business@simonandschuster.com.
Manufactured in China 0919 SDI

The year was 1926.
Nestled in paper, a critter peeked out of her box.
Shiny shoes walked toward her.

Suddenly the box top swung open.
The President and First Lady
looked down and gasped.
They were very surprised
to find a raccoon!

The First Lady frowned,
peeking into the box.
"A raccoon to eat for Thanksgiving
dinner?" she yelped.
"Not for us! We'll keep her!"

And they called her Rebecca.

Rebecca was in good company
at the White House.
President Calvin Coolidge
and his wife, Grace, loved pets.
There were so many birds
and cats and dogs.

One of the cats, Tiger,
liked to be worn as a scarf.

Knowing the Coolidges
loved all animals,
foreign leaders sent pets as gifts.
Calvin welcomed them all.

There were lion cubs
from South Africa
and thirteen Pekin ducklings!
Still, Rebecca was special.

Calvin and Grace built Rebecca
a tree house,
but she ate most of her meals
with the family.

Rebecca ate chicken, shrimp,
and a type of fruit called
persimmons (say: per-SIM-mons).
But she liked eggs the most!

At the White House Easter Egg Roll, Rebecca couldn't understand why everyone chased the eggs instead of eating them.

Rebecca loved Calvin and Grace.
Their donkey, Ebenezer, did too.

Rebecca was always waiting
for Calvin to finish his work.
He was the only one who liked
to play with her.
She tried to play with Old Bill,
Calvin's pet bird.
But Old Bill was not interested.

The wallaby from Tasmania
hopped up and down the stairs.
But raccoons aren't
made for hopping.

Calvin's bobcat, Smoky,
or the big black bear
from Mexico
might have been
Rebecca's friends . . .

but they were
never home.

Neither was Calvin's pygmy hippo,
who Calvin said swam all day
in a pond across town.

Rebecca swam in her tub all alone.

So Rebecca had to make her own fun.

She tore up
sheets,

got into
the garbage,

and chewed
on all the
President's
shoes.

“Shame on you!” scolded Grace.
“Beastly!” cried Calvin.

For the first time, the staff at the White House was grumpy. They loved the dogs and cats. They whistled with the birds.

But Rebecca did not fit in.

Sometimes Rebecca disappeared. Calvin and Grace would find her at the edges of the property.

Calvin and Grace knew
Rebecca needed a new home
with other raccoons.

They took her uptown
to a place as special as she was.

There were sticks to chew on!
There were rocks to scratch!
Rebecca chased and tumbled
and wrestled all day.
She loved her new raccoon friends.

Grace and Calvin were relieved.
And they were glad they lived
so close to the National Zoo!

• Facts About Raccoons •

• On average, raccoons are 2-3 feet long and weigh between 14 and 23 pounds.

• Wild raccoons usually live about 2-3 years, but in captivity, they can live up to 20 years.

• Raccoons eat almost anything they can find, including fruits, plants, nuts, berries, insects, frogs, and eggs. In cities, raccoons usually scavenge in the garbage for food.

• Baby raccoons are called kits, and a group of raccoons is called a gaze.

• As cute as they look, raccoons do not usually make good pets because of their mischievous nature. If you see one in your neighborhood, do not go near it. They are wild animals who love to scratch and bite, and they don't like to be contained.

• Facts About the White House •

• Theodore Roosevelt was the first to officially call the president's home the White House in 1901.

• These days, the White House has 132 rooms, including a movie theater and a bowling alley.

• There is a twin White House in Ireland called the Leinster House. Its design influenced the work of the White House's architect, James Hoban, who was born in Ireland.

• George Washington never lived in the White House. He is the only president who did not.

• The White House sits on a park of 18 acres of land. That's the size of about 13 football fields.

While the Coolidges certainly had all the pets mentioned in this book, they may not have all lived in the White House at the same time. However, Rebecca's stay at the White House probably overlapped with many of these animals.

TAILS from History

A Parrot in the Painting

THE STORY OF FRIDA KAHLO AND BONITO

By Thea Feldman

Illustrated by Rachel Sanson

Ready-to-Read

Simon Spotlight

New York London Toronto Sydney New Delhi

To Rose, who loves birds, too —T. F.

For my mum —R. S.

SIMON SPOTLIGHT
An imprint of Simon & Schuster Children's Publishing Division
1230 Avenue of the Americas, New York, New York 10020
This Simon Spotlight edition December 2019

For information about special discounts for bulk purchases, please contact
Simon & Schuster Special Sales at 1-866-506-1949 or business@simonandschuster.com.
Manufactured in China 0919 SDI

Squawk!
Bonito (say: boh-NEE-toh) the parrot flapped his wings and squawked loudly.

Bonito liked to squawk.
He had a lot to say!
He also liked to fly
around the garden
of the house where he lived.

The house was in Mexico.
It was called la Casa Azul
(say: lah KAH-sah ah-SOOL).
La Casa Azul means
“the Blue House” in Spanish.

A woman named Frida Kahlo
lived in the house.
She and her husband,
Diego Rivera, were painters.

Bonito wasn’t the only animal
who lived there.
There were cats and dogs.
Some of the dogs had no hair!

There were
spider monkeys
who climbed trees
in the garden.

There was a pretty fawn
named Granizo
(say: grah-NEE-soh).

There were lots of
other birds besides
Bonito, too.

There were little parakeets
and big macaws.

There were chickens and
an eagle.
The chickens clucked and pecked
at food grains on the ground.

Frida painted
some of these animals.

But she had not yet
painted Bonito.

In her lifetime Frida Kahlo created more than 100 paintings.

Fifty-five are self-portraits, which means they are paintings that Frida made of herself.

Frida painted herself
with one of her hairless dogs.

She painted herself with
the monkeys, a cat,
and some of the birds, too.

When was she going to
paint Bonito?

Frida promised Bonito that
she would paint him someday.

So Bonito showed Frida
just how special he was!

Bonito started performing tricks for Frida and Diego.

He twirled.
He sang.
He danced
to music.

He even made kissing sounds!

Visitors at Frida's home
were happy to watch Bonito.

As a reward,
Bonito sometimes got
a little piece of butter.

Soon, the time came for Frida to paint him!

Self-Portrait with Bonito
became one of Frida Kahlo's
most famous paintings.
Bonito and Frida,
and the bond they shared,
were captured forever!

• Facts About Amazon Parrots •

- Bonito came from a group of species called Amazon parrots. They are native to South America, Central America, and the Caribbean.
- Amazon parrots like to eat seeds, nuts, fruits, and vegetables. Butter actually isn't good for them.
- Many parrot species are endangered because people are cutting down forests and destroying the parrots' homes. Too many people are also collecting the parrots as pets.
- Humans have taste buds on their tongues, but Amazon parrots have taste buds on the roofs of their mouths.
- Amazon parrots are some of the best talkers among the more than 350 species of parrots.

• Facts About Frida Kahlo •

- Frida Kahlo was born on June 6, 1907, and died on July 13, 1954.
- Frida originally wanted to become a doctor.
- She started painting after she got into a bus accident and wanted something to do while she recovered.
- Frida's husband was Diego Rivera, an artist most famous for his murals.
- Frida's home, la Casa Azul, is now the Frida Kahlo Museum.

TAILS from History

The Cat Who Ruled the Town

By May Nakamura
Illustrated by Rachel Sanson

Ready-to-Read

Simon Spotlight
New York London Toronto Sydney New Delhi

SIMON SPOTLIGHT
An imprint of Simon & Schuster Children's Publishing Division
1230 Avenue of the Americas, New York, New York 10020
This Simon Spotlight edition December 2019

For information about special discounts for bulk purchases, please contact Simon & Schuster Special Sales at 1-866-506-1949 or business@simonandschuster.com.
Manufactured in China 0919 SDI

There is a small town in Alaska
called Talkeetna
(say: tall-KEET-nuh).
The town is so small that
fewer than nine hundred people
live there.

Most visitors pass through Talkeetna on their way to Denali (say: deh-NAH-lee). Denali is the highest mountain peak in North America.

But people also used to visit Talkeetna for another reason. They wanted to meet the mayor. Why was the mayor so special?

The mayor was a cat!

Stubbs the cat lived at
Nagley's Store.
His name was Stubbs
because he had a very short tail.

People in the town like to tell the story that in 1997, Talkeetna held an election to choose a town mayor.

The Talkeetna townspeople didn't want to vote for anyone on the ballot.
So instead they voted for Stubbs, and he won the election!

The story is just a legend.
The town is actually too small
to have a mayor and a government.
But that didn't stop people
from calling Stubbs "the mayor"!

As an honorary mayor,
Stubbs lived a very nice life.
Every afternoon
Stubbs took a break
by drinking water
from a fancy glass.

Then he sat in the store
and waited for visitors.
People from all around the world
came to the store to meet Stubbs.
Some people pretended to have
an appointment with the mayor!

Stubbs greeted these visitors by crawling onto their laps and posing for pictures.

When he got tired,
he curled up into a ball
and took a long nap.

Stubbs liked to walk around town.
He visited local restaurants,
art stores, and bakeries
to say hello to the townspeople.

The walks made Stubbs sleepy, so he would take another nap. Wherever he slept, Stubbs always left a lot of fur to clean up!

Sometimes Stubbs went to the park.
The neighborhood kids loved petting
and playing games with Stubbs.
It was great to be the town mayor!

As the years passed,
Stubbs got older.
On many days he felt too tired
to greet visitors at the store.
Stubbs had been mayor
for nineteen years.
People wondered if he would retire.

Then one summer day in 2016,
Stubbs's owners had a surprise.
"Say hello to Aurora and Denali,"
they said.
"These cats are moving in
with all of us!"

Aurora and Denali had big blue eyes
and gray and white fur.
They were barely two months old.

Stubbs had never lived
with other cats before.
He stood away and growled.

The kittens loved to play.
They tumbled, jumped,
and ran up and down the stairs.
"Meow!" said Aurora.
"Meow!" said Denali.
Stubbs hissed.

But Aurora and Denali loved Stubbs. They liked to follow him around and sleep in the same bed.

As time went on,
Stubbs grew to love
the little kittens.
Aurora and Denali were the
newest members of the family
and of Talkeetna!

The three cats became close friends. Aurora and Denali tumbled together while Stubbs swatted playfully at them. When they got tired, they all curled up and napped together.

Sometimes the two kittens joined
Stubbs at his mayoral work.
Aurora wasn't interested in meeting
all the visitors.
She didn't like to be petted.

But Denali, like Stubbs,
was great with visitors.
He loved all the attention.
He meowed, crawled onto laps,
and posed for pictures.

“Denali might become a good mayor
when he grows up!”
the people of Talkeetna
would often say.

Stubbs was happy to have new friends.

But most of all, Stubbs was happy to be loved by the people of Talkeetna . . . and the world!

· Facts About Alaska ·

• On January 3, 1959, Alaska was the forty-ninth state to become part of the United States.

• Alaska is the biggest state in the United States. It is bigger than the next three largest states—Texas, California, and Montana—combined. In terms of population, though, Alaska is the third smallest state!

• Denali, the highest mountain peak in North America, is 20,310 feet tall.

• More than ten thousand years ago, Russia and Alaska were connected by land. The Pacific Ocean separates them today.

• Alaska is the most northern state in the US. The coldest temperature ever recorded in Alaska was -80 degrees Fahrenheit in 1971. It was also the coldest temperature ever recorded in the United States!

· Facts About Cats ·

• Ancient Egyptians thought cats were magical and brought good luck. They even mummified the cats when they died!

• Cats usually have eighteen claws between their front and back paws. They retract their claws when they aren't using them.

• Cats are nocturnal, which means they are most active at night.

• Cats have great hearing. A human only has six muscles in each ear, but a cat has about thirty muscles!

• In 2016 there were almost eighty-six million pet cats in America!

TAILS from History

A Puppy for Helen Keller

By May Nakamura
Illustrated by Rachel Sanson

Ready-to-Read

Simon Spotlight
New York London Toronto Sydney New Delhi

SIMON SPOTLIGHT
An imprint of Simon & Schuster Children's Publishing Division
1230 Avenue of the Americas, New York, New York 10020
This Simon Spotlight edition December 2019

Manufactured in China 0919 SDI

In 1937, Helen Keller sailed
on a ship from America to Japan.
It was her very first time
traveling to Asia.

Helen Keller was a famous author
who could not see or hear.
Helen traveled all around the world.
She shared her stories about learning
how to read, write, and speak.
She inspired and helped many people.

A blind man named Takeo Iwahashi (say: ta-KAY-o ee-wa-HA-shee) had invited Helen to Japan. Like Helen, he wanted to help other people like him. He printed many books in braille (say: BRAYL) so that blind people could read and learn.

The Japanese people loved listening to Helen's speeches. Helen spoke about peace, respect, and understanding other people's differences.

Helen also had a special request
while she was in Japan.
She wanted to meet
an Akita (say: ah-KEE-tuh) dog!

The Akita is a dog breed
from Japan.
Ever since she was a little girl,
Helen had loved dogs.
She had owned many dogs,
but she had never owned an Akita.

Helen had read about the true story of the Akita named Hachikō (say: ha-chi-KOH).
Every evening Hachikō met his owner at the train station.
But one day Hachikō's owner did not come home after work.

More trains came and left.
Hachikō waited and waited,
but his owner never appeared.

The next day Hachikō went
to the station again.
He went the next day, and the next.
For more than nine years
Hachikō didn't give up looking
for the person he loved.

Helen was inspired by Hachikō
and his loyalty.
She wanted to meet an Akita dog.
She met a small puppy
that she nicknamed "Kami"
(say: KAH-mee).

Kami licked Helen's cheek
and cuddled in her lap.
"May I keep him?"
Helen asked.
Kami's owner said yes!

Kami traveled with Helen
to his new home in New York.
He became the first Akita
to live in the United States.

But a few months later
Kami died from a virus
that affects some dogs.
Helen was very sad.

The Japanese people were also sad to hear about Kami's death. Kami had connected Helen to Japan, but now he was gone. The Japanese people had an idea. They would send another dog to Helen!

Kenzan-Go (say: ken-zahn-GO),
or “Go-Go,”
was Kami’s brother.

Go-Go was bigger than Kami, but he was just as friendly. He would be the perfect fit for Helen!

But there was a problem.
Trouble was brewing between
Japan and the United States.

Back in 1922 both countries had promised to stop building new battleships. They wanted to focus on peace, not war.

But as time went on,
Japan changed its mind.
It started building new battleships.

Americans were worried.
Japan's army and navy were growing.
The US president was not sure
if he could trust Japan.

Some people in Japan were scared that Go-Go's trip would be unsafe. No one knew what would happen with all the trouble and distrust.

Go-Go was still ready
to meet Helen.
His ship left Japan
in the beginning of June 1939.

The journey was long and far. Go-Go's ship was surrounded by blue ocean and blue sky.

Finally the ship arrived in New York.

Would Go-Go be allowed off the ship?

"Welcome to America!"
the guard said.
And there was Helen Keller,
standing on the pier!

Go-Go ran to his new owner
and gave her a big doggy kiss.
Helen laughed.
They were so happy
to be with each other.

Helen was very grateful for the gift.
When Helen was with Go-Go,
she remembered all the kind people
she had met in Japan.

No matter what happened,
Helen would always think of
the Japanese people as her friends.
Go-Go lived a long and happy life
with Helen Keller.
Nothing could separate an
Akita and its owner.

· Facts About Akita Dogs ·

- Akitas are strong and powerful. They used to be popular hunting dogs!
- Akitas get their name from the Akita region in northern Japan.
- Akitas have webbed toes. This makes it easier for them to walk on snow.
- In Japan the Akita dog is considered a national treasure.
- Hachikō is still very famous today. Movies have been made and books have been written about his story. In Tokyo there is also a famous Hachikō statue at the Shibuya (say: shee-BU-ya) train station. The statue is a popular meeting spot.

· Facts About Helen Keller ·

- Helen Keller was born on June 27, 1880, and died on June 1, 1968.
- She became blind and deaf when she was nineteen months old.
- Helen was the first blind and deaf person to graduate from college.
- Helen traveled to Japan with her companion, Polly Thomson. One of the ways they communicated with each other was spelling words onto the other person's palm.
- Helen visited Japan again in 1948 and 1955.

TAILS from History

A Sea Otter to the Rescue

By Thea Feldman

Illustrated by Rachel Sanson

Ready-to-Read

Simon Spotlight

New York London Toronto Sydney New Delhi

SIMON SPOTLIGHT
An imprint of Simon & Schuster Children's Publishing Division
1230 Avenue of the Americas, New York, New York 10020
This Simon Spotlight edition December 2019

Manufactured in China 0919 SDI

It was a summer day in 2001.
There was a new sea otter
at an aquarium in California.

The sea otter's name was Toola.
Toola was a grown-up sea otter—
about five years old.
She was sick because of cat litter
that had been dumped into the ocean.
Toola needed medicine every day
to stay healthy.

The aquarium rescues sick sea otters
because they are endangered
(say: en-DANE-jurd).
That means they are at risk
of disappearing forever.
There are only about three thousand
wild sea otters living in California.

The aquarium took good care
of Toola.
She quickly settled into
her new home.
She liked to make the staff
chase her in the water.

Soon after, a rescued baby sea otter was brought into the aquarium. A baby sea otter is called a pup.

This pup was an orphan.
No one knew what had happened to his mother.

He was only two weeks old.
That is much too young
for a pup to be on his own.

In the past,
some of the aquarium staff
had raised sea otters.
The humans had become parents
for the orphaned pups.

When the pups were ready
to return to the ocean,
the staff put tags
on the pups' flippers.
This way, the aquarium could track
the otters in the wild.

However, very few of these sea otters lived long in the wild.
Maybe it was because they had spent too much time with humans.

This time, the staff had an idea. What if they gave the new orphaned pup to Toola? She was old enough to be a mother.

No one knew what would happen if they paired a pup with another sea otter. Would Toola raise the pup as her own?

The pup floated on his back.
He didn't know how to swim.
Toola swam up to him.
She reached toward the pup
with her front paws.

Then she pulled him onto her chest,
just like any mother otter would do.
Toola had adopted the pup!

Toola was a good mother.
She opened clamshells
and shared them with the pup.

When the pup was ready,
Toola taught him how to swim.
She pulled him along in the water
and encouraged him
to use his flippers.

She taught him how to dive, too.
Sea otters have to dive
to find their food.
They like to eat shellfish,
such as clams and crabs,
that live on the ocean floor.

Toola showed the pup
how to open a hard shell.
She put a rock on her chest.
Then she hit the shell against
the rock until the shell cracked!

She even taught the pup
how to make sure a crab
would not pinch his nose!

A sea otter's fur keeps it warm
and dry in the water.
The fur must always stay clean,
so Toola spent many hours every day
cleaning the pup's fur.

Then Toola showed him
how to groom his fur.
She rubbed and licked her own fur.
She turned over and over
in the water.

When the pup was about
six months old, he was ready
to return to the ocean.
The staff tracked the pup
with a tag. They watched him
grow up in the wild and
have many pups of his own!

Toola had taught the pup
to be a great sea otter!
She had done what no sea otter
at the aquarium had done before.

Toola stayed at the aquarium
to continue taking her medicine.
She raised twelve more pups.
She went from being rescued
by the aquarium staff
to rescuing other sea otters!

There are now many sea otters
who raise orphaned pups
at the aquarium.

A young boy heard about Toola. His dad was a lawmaker in California. He asked his dad to write a law to protect sea otters. The law passed in 2006. It allows people to donate money to the endangered sea otters.

People have donated more than
three million dollars,
thanks to Toola!

The law helps scientists
who study sea otters.
This way, the scientists can learn
how to protect them in the wild.

Toola lived to be fifteen or sixteen years old. She was always busy raising pups or just having fun. Toola had no idea she was the most important sea otter in the aquarium's history!

Facts about Sea Otters

- Toola was a southern sea otter. They live along the coast of California.
- Sea otters are the largest members of the weasel family.
- Sea otters can hold their breath for up to five minutes.
- Sea otters sleep while floating on their backs.
- Humans have about a hundred thousand hairs on their heads. Sea otters can have up to one million hairs per square inch. That is the most fur per square inch of any animal!

How You Can Help Sea Otters

- Throw away your trash properly. Litter can pollute the ocean.
- Write to your lawmakers and ask them to help protect sea otters and other marine life.
- If you ever see a sea otter, keep your distance. They may be cute, but touching them is unsafe for the otter and for you.
- If you have a pet cat, don't flush the cat litter down the drain. Cat litter contains bacteria that makes sea otters sick.
- Spread the word about sea otters. Tell your family and friends how they can help too!

TAILS from History

A Pony with Her Writer

THE STORY OF MARGUERITE HENRY AND MISTY

By Thea Feldman
Illustrated by Rachel Sanson

Ready-to-Read

Simon Spotlight
New York London Toronto Sydney New Delhi

SIMON SPOTLIGHT
An imprint of Simon & Schuster Children's Publishing Division
1230 Avenue of the Americas, New York, New York 10020
This Simon Spotlight edition December 2019

For information about special discounts for bulk purchases, please contact Simon & Schuster Special Sales at 1-866-506-1949 or business@simonandschuster.com.
Manufactured in China 0919 SDI

It was July 1946. Something very special was happening on Chincoteague (say: SHING-kuh-teeg) Island in Virginia.

It was an event called
the Pony Penning.
Thousands of people
were gathered along the shore.

Then they started cheering.
In the distance they could see
ponies swimming in the ocean!

Right next to Chincoteague
is an island called Assateague
(say: AAH-suh-teeg).
Many wild ponies live there.

For most of the year
these ponies run free.
They eat grass and
drink a lot of fresh water.

However, during the Pony Penning the townspeople gather up some of the wild ponies. They all walk to the shore.

Then the ponies swim
from Assateague Island
to Chincoteague Island!

Once they reach Chincoteague,
the ponies gallop through the town.

People attend the Pony Penning from all over the world.
Marguerite Henry was one of those people in 1946.
She wrote books for children and was looking for new story ideas.

While Marguerite was at the Pony Penning, she heard about a beautiful pony named Misty. Marguerite decided to visit the Beebe family, who owned Misty.

Misty was still a baby pony,
which is called a "foal."
She had many white markings
on her hair.

One marking looked like
the United States turned sideways.
There were many ponies
on Chincoteague Island,
but only one pony looked like this!

Marguerite was dazzled by Misty's beauty.
She wanted to take Misty home and write a story about her.

Marguerite offered to write about the Beebe family in her story too.
The Beebes thought that was a great idea!

They agreed that Marguerite could borrow Misty.
But when Misty was old enough to have her own foals, she would need to return home.

Marguerite returned to her farm in Illinois. That winter she received a pony from Chincoteague. But this pony didn't look like Misty. She looked more like a goat!

Marguerite thought that the Beebes had sent the wrong pony. Marguerite was sad but loved the new pony anyway.

The pony settled into
her new home. She liked
eating carrots and
munching on oats.

Finally spring arrived.
The pony shed her winter coat . . .
and revealed her white markings!
The pony was Misty after all!

Meanwhile, Marguerite had been busy writing her new book. In 1947 she published *Misty of Chincoteague*. The story was based on everything that Marguerite had seen at the Pony Penning.

The book became very popular.
Many people wanted to meet Misty.
She visited museums,
school assemblies,
and libraries for story hour.

Misty shook hooves with her fans.
She liked having her ears scratched
and her neck stroked.
She liked all the carrot treats too!

One time Misty and Marguerite
were invited to a conference
for librarians.
It was on the seventh floor.
Misty rode her very first elevator!

Back at home Misty had many friends. She lived with a horse called Friday and a cat called Mom-cat. There was also Brighty the donkey, who inspired another one of Marguerite's books.

Every year Marguerite held
a birthday party for Misty.
Many children attended the parties.
They gave presents to Misty.

In 1957, Misty was old enough
to have her own foals.
Marguerite loved living with Misty,
but she needed to keep her promise.
It was time for Misty to go home.

Misty's farewell party was
her biggest party ever. There were
more than three hundred guests.
She even had a cake
with carrots for candles!

Misty returned to Chincoteague
and became a mother
to three beautiful foals.

Marguerite missed Misty,
but she knew that the pony
belonged in Chincoteague.
No matter where they were,
Marguerite and Misty would
always be connected by
the book *Misty of Chincoteague*!

Facts About Chincoteague Ponies

- Most of the wild Chincoteague ponies do not actually live on Chincoteague Island. Instead they live on the nearby Assateague Island.
- The Chincoteague ponies on the island are feral. That means that a long time ago, they used to be domestic and live among humans, but today they are wild.
- The Pony Penning still takes place every year in July.
- During the Pony Penning, some people buy ponies to take home. This way, the wild ponies that stay on Assateague Island have enough food to eat.
- Wild ponies stick together in small groups called "bands."

Facts About Marguerite Henry

- Marguerite Henry was born on April 13, 1902, and died on November 26, 1997.
- When Marguerite was a young girl, she enjoyed visiting her father's printing shop.
- Marguerite also wrote stories about other ponies, including one called *Stormy, Misty's Foal.*
- Marguerite had her first magazine article published when she was eleven years old.
- Marguerite wrote fifty-nine books during her lifetime.